The
Outlaw

By C. W. Anderson

The
Outlaw

by C. W. ANDERSON

THE MACMILLAN COMPANY, NEW YORK
COLLIER-MACMILLAN LIMITED, LONDON

*To the memory
of James Rarey*

Contents

The
Outlaw

1 Father and Son

The phone rang and then rang again. The tall, lean man got up from the breakfast table, the heels of his cowboy boots sounding sharply on the bare kitchen floor.

"Three?" he said into the phone. "I'll see what we can do. We have two that are ready but we'd like a little more time on that blaze-faced bay. We'll do the best we can. Thanks, Jim."

He came back to the table and picked up his cup.

"They want three more horses for the Bar O Dude Ranch. Gentle and foolproof. Suppose you give White Face all your time this week. He's still a little skittish and might buck with a poor rider. We're doing so well we can't afford to have anything go wrong now, Janon."

"White Face will be all right," said the boy. "There's nothing mean or tricky about him—he's just nervous. As if he doesn't know what will happen next. Someone must have been mighty rough with him. It took a long time to get him to trust me."

"I know. That's the tough part of our job. We have to

take the spoiled ones and make them over. If only we could afford a bigger spread and raise our own stock we would be in clover."

"Maybe some day we'll get a break, Dad. Still, we get good prices. People know they can count on our horses. Not many folks would spend the time with a horse that we do. Not out here, anyway. And then you are the best at gentling a horse that there is."

"I try, Janon, but I'll never be as good as Grandfather was. He was really a wonder. It was almost as if he and horses talked the same language. He'd take a horse nobody could handle and have him gentle in a week. He always wanted to be off by himself with a horse he worked with, so nobody knew just what he did. All we knew was that he was quiet and gentle with them, never raised his voice. You could see he was always talking to them but it must have been very softly for you never heard a word. Just kept patting them and moving very slowly around them." Mr. Kendricks paused, his mind far away, remembering.

"He said he was going to teach me someday when I was a little older. I guess he thought there was plenty of time but there wasn't. So nobody ever knew just what he did. Not all of it."

Mr. Kendricks stood at the corral rail and watched his son work with the blaze-faced bay. First Janon had him at a slow, easy lope, around and around, then pulled him to a walk on a loose rein. The bay stopped on the command while Janon dismounted, spoke to the horse quietly and then mounted. Mr. Kendricks noted how the horse stood quietly after the boy was in the saddle.

"He's a natural horseman," he thought as he watched the slim youngster handling the horse on the lightest of reins. All the boys his age couldn't wait to get their first spurs and be bronc riders. Make them buck even if they didn't want to. Janon never cared for all that. He really loved horses and always thought of *them*, didn't try to show off.

How many times Mr. Kendricks had heard these callow youngsters boast that they could "ride anything that wore hair." He smiled to himself. Janon could come nearer doing that than any of them but he chose to do it his own way. What horses he and Janon could turn out if only they could start from scratch with horses they had raised themselves that had never had any rough handling. Nothing to forget before they could start to learn.

A small sigh escaped him as he turned toward the low stable.

"He's a natural horseman," he thought as he watched the slim youngster handling the horse on the lightest of reins. All the boys his age couldn't wait to get their first spurs and be bronc riders. Janon never cared for all that.

4

2 "The Whisperer"

The rain came down in a steady sheet of water—one of those deluges that often follow a prolonged dry spell. The horses were under cover and nothing could be done outdoors. Janon decided to straighten up the attic. So much had accumulated in that low space under the rafters. It was all piled haphazardly, as one year's discards followed another. Taking a flashlight he went up the dark, steep stairs. The rain pounded and surged on the low roof with the sound of Dry River in flood.

Janon flashed his light around the dark corners beyond the familiar things—several old trunks, a discarded chair, a broken-down dresser—and his eye caught something back under the eaves he hadn't noticed before. It was a small wooden box tied with a piece of twine. He got it out to the middle of the floor. The twine was so old it fell apart at his touch. On top of the hinged lid were the letters J N K burned into the wood as if with a hot iron. This must have belonged to his great-grandfather, for whom he was named.

He lifted the lid and on top of some very old books lay a

folded newspaper, yellow with age. The headline read "The Whisperer Dies."

Carefully he carried the box downstairs. Finding a place by a window he picked up the paper. *The Irish Field*, he saw at the top of the page. Then he began reading.

"James Sullivan, called 'The Whisperer,' died today. He gained fame for an uncanny ability to tame vicious horses, even killers, in a remarkably short time. No one knew his method for he never let anyone see him at work. He had a large stable where he took the horse and stayed with it for many hours, sometimes all day. When he finally brought it out it was an entirely different animal. His fame spread throughout all Ireland and there is no case on record where he ever failed with a horse.

"Some boys who stole up to the stable and peered through a crack reported that he only seemed to stroke the horse and speak to him constantly in a very soft voice. Hence his name, 'The Whisperer.' As he never divulged his secret it went with him to the grave."

Janon laid the paper carefully on the table for it was brittle with age. This was something his great-grandfather had saved—something he valued. It had been marked carefully around the edges with ink and the line "He only seemed to stroke the horse and speak to him constantly in a very soft voice" was strongly underlined.

Janon sat staring at the streaming window. What if it was as simple as that? Only carried much further than any-

one had ever thought of. Much further. He read the story once more. "Many hours," it said. Suddenly Janon recalled how a few minutes of petting a nervous horse and talking to it quietly had settled it down. And that was only minutes!

His father came in, taking off a dripping raincoat and hat. He noticed the box on the table and ran his fingers over the letters burned in the lid.

"This must have been Grandfather's," he said. "Where did you find it?"

"Up in the attic. Way off in a dark corner. I'd never have seen it without a flashlight. Look at this, Dad," and he handed the old paper to him.

Mr. Kendricks read it slowly. Then he sat for a while in deep thought.

"I remember he spoke of The Whisperer," he said at last. "Said that out here nobody would understand a man like that. 'All whips and spurs,' he said. 'That's all they know.' "

"Do you suppose that's what Great-grandfather did, too? What The Whisperer did? Maybe that's why he wanted to be off by himself. So people wouldn't laugh at him for being so slow and gentle."

This was something his great-grandfather had saved—something he valued. It had been marked carefully around the edges with ink and the line "He only seemed to stroke the horse and speak to him constantly in a very soft voice" was strongly underlined.

"You may be right, Son. Those were tough days for a horse. 'Show him who's boss' was the idea. Whips, spurs, even clubs. They'd never understand a man like Grandfather. You know he never would sell a horse to a man until he saw him handle it. No matter what the price."

"Oh, he was right," said Janon. "That's the way it should be. I wish I had known him."

"He would have liked you. You're like him—very much like him."

"But not enough, Dad. Not nearly enough. But I'll try to be."

3 The Outlaw

Janon was in the corral working a sorrel mare. His father came up to him and stroked the mare's head.

"She's different," he said. "Quieter and more gentle. Is that what you did with White Face too? They called up and said all the youngsters are crazy about that horse."

Janon's face lighted up. "It works, Dad! It's simple but it really works. You just can't believe it. After a while you see their fear and nervousness just melt away. You can feel it through your hands."

"But if it's that simple why hasn't everyone done it? Many people like horses."

"I think it's the time. You remember what it said about The Whisperer: 'hours, sometimes all day.' Maybe it's only with a lot of time that you get through to a horse if he's been handled badly. Let him know things will be different."

Kendricks looked at Janon very seriously. "Do you think it would always work? Even with a really bad actor—an outlaw?"

11

"I think so, Dad. It seems such a simple thing but I really believe it would work."

"I hope you're right. You'll get a chance to try. I took a gamble on the grandest-looking horse I ever saw. Over at the Double S. Nobody could ride him and the bronc rider they brought in is in the hospital with a broken leg. So they wanted to get rid of him. I got him cheap; cheap, if we ever can do anything with him."

"I saw a big black in their corral when I went by the other day. High-headed and full of fire."

"That's him. They say he is as mean as he is handsome. Maybe he is. Maybe he *is* a real outlaw. If he is we may be licked. But let's just put him in the big corral. Feed him and leave him alone. Try to get him to feel he's on his own. Never make a move—wait for him to come to you. It may take time—maybe it will never happen—but that's the only way. He's really been through the mill, that horse. Marks of spurs, quirts, ropes: everything. And one look at his eye and you know that's not for him. Not so long as he has a leg under him."

"It sounds pretty tough," said Janon.

"It is," said Mr. Kendricks. "About as tough as I ever saw." He was quiet for a moment. "But you know, Son, maybe once in your life you see a horse that you know is the one. The best you could imagine. This is the one!"

At last they had the black in the corral. It had been a job—a real day's work. He had fought so, that the only way they could handle him was with two long ropes, Janon and his father riding fifty feet apart with the black horse between them. Even then progress was slow for he reared, bucked and fought every yard of the way.

Standing alone in the middle of the corral, his black body wet and lathered, he snorted his defiance through distended nostrils. His eyes flashed fire, the white in them much in evidence. He looked every inch the wild horse that had never known the touch of man, only bigger and handsomer than any of them.

"What a strange star he has!" exclaimed Janon. "A perfect diamond, isn't it?"

"Yes," said his father. "I've never seen one quite like that. And seldom so big a star, especially with not another white hair on him. Nobody would ever forget him once they saw him."

They stood and studied the horse silently for some time. "There's mighty little cold blood there," said Mr. Kendricks. "You don't see that conformation in broncs. He's probably clean bred."

"You mean Thoroughbred?" asked Janon.

His father nodded. "They didn't know his breeding over at the Double S. They thought he might be of quarter horse strain with enough speed to make a cutting horse. They knew he was tough but thought they could break him. He fooled them plenty."

Janon could not take his eyes off the shining black horse. "He looks different from any I've seen," he said at last.

"Everything seems to fit so. And then his coat. Did you ever see a coat shine so?"

"That's the Thoroughbred. They've been cared for and groomed generation after generation. Our broncs are out in all sorts of weather so they've grown a coarser coat for protection—helps keep out the wet. You don't see this sort out here. I wonder where he came from."

After Janon threw in a few forkfuls of hay he kept standing very still by the corral fence. At first the black would not come near the hay while Janon was there but soon it was too tempting, for the grass was very sparse in the corral. Since the boy remained motionless the horse soon took him for granted and was no longer nervous about his presence. Occasionally he raised his head and looked at Janon curiously.

"This horse is used to grain and he needs it," said his father one day. "Some folks think you can starve the spirit out of a horse but underfeeding can make a horse even more nervous. Start giving him a couple of quarts of grain morning and night. He'll look for it and since you're the one who brings it to him he may begin to let down his guard a little. But let him come to you. He's got to

The only way they could handle him was with two long ropes, Janon and his father riding fifty feet apart with the black horse between them.

15

make up his mind about you first. Don't make a move."

The eagerness with which the black horse pushed the feed tub around searching for the last bit of grain made Janon realize how much it meant to the horse. So eager was he for the grain that he came at once and seemed unaware of the boy who stood so quietly beside him.

At exactly the same time each day the black came to the corral gate and gave a shrill whinny. "He's sure got a clock in his head," thought Janon. "He knows when it's feeding time. I won't keep him waiting. If he knows I always come when he calls it may help."

As the days went by Janon felt that he and the black horse understood each other. Now Janon always remained standing beside the horse while he ate. It was hard not to reach out and stroke that smooth, dark shoulder but he knew his father was right. He spoke softly to him about what they would one day do together. Occasionally the horse would raise his head and almost seem to listen. Once he brought his head over as if to rub against Janon, but then drew back.

"Never make a move," his father had said. "Let him come to you." It was hard to wait but Janon knew it was the only way.

16

4 James Rarey

"He turned to me today and touched my hand," said Janon as they sat down to a lunch of beans and bacon. Janon and his father took turns cooking as they had ever since Mrs. Kendricks' death three years before. Left to shift for themselves they did the best they could with the simplest of cooking.

"That's really something," said his father leaning forward and speaking earnestly. "I thought it would take much longer. To some people that would seem nothing at all but it means he knows you and is beginning to trust you. Now you can pat him, but never push it. He must meet you halfway."

"He looks for his grain so much and that helped. He seems to like me to stand beside him and talk to him." He hesitated. "You know in one of those books of Great-grand-father's it said you could do a lot with a horse if you stroked it very gently. 'As if it were a hummingbird.'"

"Was that Rarey?" asked his father. Janon nodded.

"Grandfather saw him once when he was a young boy.

He often spoke of it. Rarey took a wild-eyed stallion that two men could scarcely handle and in an hour rode it bareback with only a halter. It doesn't seem possible but he did it again and again. I think Grandfather used his ideas when he worked with horses."

"Did you read the whole book on Rarey, Dad? About Cruiser? That nobody dared go near the horse for months? Even though he wore a heavy muzzle. And Rarey had them open up the heavy oak door and he walked right in. They all expected him to be dead in a few minutes. Then he walked out with Cruiser. And rode that horse to London a few days later. It has to be true. It was in all the papers. But how did he do it? How could he ever do it?"

"He was a strange man, Son. A missionary, really. Only his field was horses. He really loved them and there was never a horse that lived that he feared. In some way that must have come through to them. Horses hate the smell of fear in a man, and it has a smell, Son. Strong and acrid. And always with that comes violence and abuse. They know that."

Janon was thoughtful and was turning things over in his mind. "Do you think that was it? That and his gentleness? They say he only stroked those tough horses and talked to them. It doesn't seem possible that only that would do it."

"He turned to me today and touched my hand."

19

"Nobody ever did it as he did. How much time does the average person take in patting and talking to a horse? Maybe a minute or two—no more. How long do you talk to a man before you know if you can trust him—see if he thinks as you do? Hours and maybe days. Horses are people, Son. A little nicer and a little more dependable, maybe, but people."

5 The Prairie Fire

Janon had just come out of the stable with the feed bucket when he heard a high whinny and the drum of hoofs. The black had been looking for him and came at a gallop toward the gate. Janon's face lighted up.

"It's mostly the grain," he thought, "but I think he likes me too." He stroked the sleek shoulder as the horse ate and there came a surge of happiness as he felt the muscles slide beneath his hand. There was such a feeling of power! He was like that all through his body as Janon well knew. He had stroked him and talked to him quietly. There seemed a relaxation of tension as the horse nuzzled him.

"Some day I'll ride you," he said softly. "When you know me well enough to trust me. You'll tell me when."

The black raised his head and rubbed it against Janon's shoulder. His eye was dark and clear, not mild—for there was that inner fire that would never be quenched—but the white no longer showed in the eye.

Janon snapped the lead rope to the halter and opened the corral gate. The black had been so obedient that Janon

felt he could safely take him out to graze on the open range near home. Although he was always fed good hay Janon knew that a horse craves the green that he can crop in the open. It seems to have a special flavor that he craves.

The black raised his head and snorted with quivering nostrils when he saw open range before him, but he made no effort to get away. He followed eagerly as Janon led him on. A nibble here and a mouthful there and he seemed happy and content. A high wind ruffled his mane and carried his tail behind him like a banner. Janon, watching, felt a shiver run through him. "He looks like a king," he thought, "just like a king ought to look. That's what I'll call him, King, if Dad agrees."

They wandered farther and farther over the prairie and when Janon looked back their ranch house was like a small toy on the horizon. "We'd better start back, Boy," he said. Suddenly the horse lifted his head with a whistling snort. Janon turned his head in the same direction and the smell of smoke came on the wind. A faint haze showed in the distance. Janon knew what that meant. A prairie fire —and with this wind it would travel like an express train! He turned and started at a run with the black galloping beside him and pulling him along. All horses fear fire but none so much as those brought up on the prairie.

Pulling the black almost to a stop he vaulted to his back. In an instant the horse was off at a full gallop.

A quick glance over his shoulder and he could see the leaping flames as a clump of sagebrush, tinder dry, flamed up. . . . It was coming even faster than he had feared. The ranch was still far away and they must reach the firebreak his father had plowed around their place for such an emergency. There was no time to be lost.

Pulling the black almost to a stop he vaulted to his back. In an instant the horse was off at a full gallop. Janon clung to his mane and gripped as hard as he could with his knees for he had never felt such speed. Tears came to his eyes as his hair whipped wildly around his face. Before he realized it they were over the plowed furrows of the firebreak, which the black cleared in a flying leap that all but left Janon airborne. The horse slid to a stop before the corral. "You were wonderful, Boy," said Janon as he led him into the stable. Then he hurried out to help his father take care of any sparks that might have leaped the firebreak.

"And you rode him bareback?" said Mr. Kendricks later. "You didn't think about the top bronc rider being thrown?"

"There wasn't time to think of anything but getting away from the fire. I guess that's all he thought of too. He knew that was no time for fighting and bucking."

"That's right. He's no outlaw. Only a rebel. He has to see a reason for things. This time he did. Try to keep it that way."

6 King of Diamonds

Mr. Kendricks came to the corral and watched Janon riding the black horse, bareback and with only a hackamore.

"Do you think that's the answer?" he said.

"I'm not sure," said Janon. "Since he let me up on him going from the fire I thought I'd go along that way. I don't want to show him a saddle and bridle yet."

"And you talk to him?"

"Always," said Janon. "You wouldn't believe how it settles him down when he's nervous. All I have to do is to stroke his neck and talk to him very softly." He hesitated, and then went on. "Do you know, Dad, I really believe it's the gentleness that does it? At first he looked surprised and then you'd feel him relax all over."

Mr. Kendricks seemed deep in thought. "That may be the whole answer," he said at last. "It's so simple that it doesn't seem possible. Maybe that's why Grandfather waited to tell me. It was too simple for a child to understand."

"What shall we call him, Janon?" said his father that night at supper. "He ought to have a name—a good name."

Janon hesitated. "When I had him out there on the range and he stood looking around with his head so high and the wind blowing his mane and tail he looked so—sort of noble. Like a king. How would King be?"

"If it hadn't been used so much it would be fine. But so many horses have been called King—even very poor ones." Then seeing the disappointment in Janon's face he added quickly, "Still we might use it in a way. With that big diamond for a star we could call him King of Diamonds."

"I like that. It sounds like a name a good race horse would have."

His father looked up sharply. "Race horse?" he said.

"I rode him away from the fire, Dad. I've been up on lots of horses but nothing like that. Nothing anywhere near like that."

"That's what he was bred for. And from what I saw it came through. But all his speed won't do any good unless we can get his papers to prove he's a Thoroughbred. He can't race at any good track without them."

"But why is that, Dad? If he's fast enough why can't he race?"

Mr. Kendricks came to the corral and watched Janon riding the black horse, bareback and with only a hackamore.

26

"Because only the Thoroughbred has the sort of speed you need for racing. Add any other blood and you lose some of the speed. So the rule was made to keep off the horses that would merely clutter up the track."

"How will we ever find his papers when we don't even know where he came from?"

"Well, I'm certain he's a Thoroughbred. He has to be with all that speed and his conformation. Then it's ten to one his sire is black—the color usually comes from the stallion. So we look for a ranch that is standing a black Thoroughbred stallion."

"How would we go about that?"

"They're all listed. I'll check and find out. Blacks are not too common. That will narrow things down a little. Then we'll look for a Thoroughbred mare that's been bred to one of them. She'll be dark—probably brown or black with a big star. Any white around the head almost always comes through to the foal, so she'd be sure to have a very big star."

Janon looked at his father admiringly. "You'd be a good detective, Dad. That certainly sounds a lot simpler. How do we start?"

"I'll check and locate the black stallions in this part of the country. Then we'll start from there."

"If we can find his papers so he can race and if he's fast enough to win we might have enough to get some extra land and mares and all that."

28

"Whoa, Son! You're going pretty fast. There are a lot of 'ifs' in that."

"Still it could happen, couldn't it?"

"Sure. And we might also find gold on our land."

"Not gold, Dad. But maybe a diamond. A really big diamond might do it."

7 Frontier Day

Ever since they came back from town that afternoon Mr. Kendricks had been preoccupied and withdrawn. Janon noticed it but knew his father would tell him what was on his mind when he was ready. Maybe it was something he had to think out first.

At supper it was the same, his father scarcely noticing what he ate. Finally Janon could stand it no longer.

"What is it, Dad? What is bothering you?"

His father looked up and said, "I heard in town those two sections to the north of us are for sale. Those're the ones we've always wanted—the ones we'd need if we were ever to expand and raise our own stock."

"What's the price?" asked Janon anxiously.

"Five thousand," said his father. "I couldn't raise that without taking a mortgage on this place and that's something I won't risk. But at that price somebody is sure to take it soon."

"Wouldn't they take a down payment and give you time on the rest?"

30

"Two thousand down is the best they'll do. The bank is handling it and they're tough. I can raise fifteen hundred but that's all. Even if we could get hold of the rest what would we do when the balance was due? Ninety days is all they'll allow."

"But we've got to get that land, Dad. It's our only chance to get the spread we need. The Bar O would never sell any of theirs."

Then Janon said, "Maybe this might be a starter." And he unfolded a handbill he took from his pocket. At the top in large black letters was printed "Frontier Day." There followed a list of events and then, also in large type, "Quarter Horse Race, $500 First Prize."

His father read it and looked up. "You mean the black? And we've never even had a saddle on him!"

"He's ready for a saddle, now, Dad. I've had a surcingle and blanket on to get him used to the girth. He didn't mind after the first time, when he saw it wouldn't hurt him. And he really trusts me now. I'll have him ready for the saddle by then."

"They'll be sending in some good quarter horses and experienced riders. You and the black are both green hands."

"All I'll have to do is stay with him. He'll do the rest. I know he will."

"I'll be cheering for you but you'll have a man-sized job ahead of you."

31

"I'll have the King of Diamonds, Dad. Maybe there isn't an ace around."

Janon had made inquiries and found that the quarter horse race was the last event of the afternoon after the rodeo was over. So they planned to bring in the black as late as possible.

"You know, Dad, he's not really a spooky horse—the sort that'll shy at his own shadow. You'd think he would be, the way he acted when we first got him, but he doesn't scare easily. He's tough—a real fighter."

"That's the way I've sized him up. You've got to have him on your side or you're never going anywhere."

"He is—so far," said Janon after a moment.

His father looked at him keenly. "You're wondering if it's far enough. When they line up at the start he's got to want to run. Otherwise it's all off."

Janon nodded, his face worried.

"Look at it this way, Son. He's bred to run; it's in the blood, has been for centuries. Just that and nothing else. When the horses line up at the start he'll know what it's for. Even if he's never been near a race track. With all those horses snorting and pawing and fighting to be off he'll know. And unless I miss my guess, he won't want another horse ahead of him as long as he can draw a breath."

"He doesn't scare easily. He's tough—a real fighter."

8 The Quarter Horse Race

There were a dozen or more horses milling around where a stake marked the start of the race. Far down the stretch the crowd was gathered near the corral where the rodeo had been held. The race was a quarter of a mile straightaway with the finish at the corral.

"Now get in line," called the starter. "Don't any of you try to get a jump or I'll fine you. You, boy, on that black. Take him to the outside so he'll settle down."

Most of the riders were cowboys with western saddles, but one crafty-faced fellow was riding a racing saddle and he had a look about him that made Janon decide to stay out of his way. He kept edging up and caused several false starts until the starter called out, "Try that again and it will cost you ten dollars."

At last the horses were more or less in line—as near in line as such a seething mass could ever be. The starter shouted: "Go!"

In that thundering charge all that Janon was aware of was that his horse was running with such a surge of power that he had all he could do to stay with him. Dust stung his eyes and blinded him to everything around at first but as it cleared he could see that the black was right with the leaders and only the hard-faced jockey on the race horse was ahead of them. A thrill ran through him as he realized how freely and willingly King was running and Janon felt that he could still let out another notch if urged. He would soon find out.

Now they were near enough so that he could clearly see the crowd at the finish and hear the cheering. This was the time to go after the bay horse ahead.

"Come on, King! Come on, Boy!" cried Janon, crouching lower over the withers, and his voice rose in excitement. "Let's go and get him!"

The effect was so sudden that Janon was scarcely prepared for it. In a half dozen tremendous strides the black drove up to the bay's girth. Janon saw the angry, twisted face of the jockey as his arm rose and he lashed with his whip, catching King a stinging blow across the nose. The horse broke his stride and seemed to falter, then came again in a wild rush. He drove up and reached over with bared teeth and wild flashing eyes as they came up to the bay. He missed the jockey's leg by a hair and then they were by. Janon saw fear in the jockey's face as he jerked on the reins to pull his horse aside. King surged on and over the finish line two lengths ahead.

Anger seethed in Janon. Unfairness of any kind brought

up a hot anger in him that was usually under control. Now if he could have gotten his hands on that fellow it would have been bad for him. What if that blow with the whip had undone all his careful work?

It took all Janon's efforts to bring the black to a halt. His eyes were still wild with anger and his nostrils quivering. At first he paid no attention to Janon's voice or the hand that stroked him so gently. They had gone a long way beyond the finish before he could be turned back, and then he was tense and jumpy. Janon realized how tight he was wound up—right to the breaking point. He turned him toward home. He must get him away from that place and all memory of it as soon as possible. His father would understand.

Janon never took his hand away from King's neck, and in a soft voice talked to him—told him how wonderful he was. After a few miles he felt a slight lessening of tension under his hand, and there was a little less white in the eye; from the flaring nostrils he only snorted occasionally. Gradually the stride became smoother and longer. When Janon felt this he pulled up and slid to the ground. Hurriedly he examined King's head. The mark of the whip was there—a slight welt where it had caught the horse right over the nose.

Janon saw the angry, twisted face of the jockey as his arm rose and he lashed with his whip, catching King a stinging blow across the nose.

With the gentlest possible touch Janon stroked the head and softly rubbed away the mark of the whip as well as he could. Now was the time to think of Rarey's advice. "Stroke him as gently as if he were a hummingbird." At first the black pulled away but soon the gentle touch seemed to soothe him. So the boy and horse stood for a long time as the sun sank lower over the far hills. The sound of a car aroused them and Mr. Kendricks' truck came in sight far down the road. Soon it was beside them.

As he got out of the truck his father handed Janon an envelope. "They sent you this and asked me to tell you how sorry they were for what happened. That fellow just kept going. If he hadn't they would have given him a rough time. They were all boiling mad."

He turned to the horse and touched his head gently. "Do you think it did much harm?" he asked. "Something he won't forget?"

"I don't know, Dad. It won't change him with us, I'm sure. But do you think he'll ever trust a horse and rider beside him again? In a race, I mean?"

"That's something we'll have to find out. We know now that he can really run. If we can get his papers I'll gamble on a down payment on that land. When you've got one like this you've got a straight flush right to the king. In diamonds. There isn't much that beats that."

⑨ The Thoroughbred Papers

Janon and his father were sitting at the breakfast table over their second cup of coffee. The race of yesterday had been rerun many times during breakfast.

"You don't feel that King would 'clutter up the track' if he went in a real race?" asked Janon with a grin.

"I said that about those 'almost race horses.' So many people have one. 'Fast as the wind and they could run any of those pampered Thoroughbreds right into the ground.' If someone like that had money enough he could enter his horse in the Derby just to see his colors up. Might mess up the chances of a really good horse. That's why they have the rule."

"I know, Dad. We've got to get his papers. When do we start?"

"I've checked on the stallions," his father said, taking a paper out of his pocket. "There are only three blacks that are Thoroughbreds in this part of the country. I've marked the routes on this map and I figure it will take two days' driving to cover them. There may be some things coming up that I should handle so I'm going to let you make the trip. I guess you know what to do."

"I think so. Look for a Thoroughbred mare that had a black colt by one of them. One with a big diamond star. If he's registered get his papers."

"Right, Son. Why not start early tomorrow? Then in a few days we'll know if we can risk that down payment."

Janon got slowly out of the truck. He had driven many miles in covering all of the ranches and was very discouraged. No Thoroughbred mares were in this area. The Thoroughbred stallions had been donated by breeding organizations to improve the local stock. This was the last chance and he felt that the story here would be the same.

The man at the stable shook his head at Janon's questions, but as the boy turned wearily away he said, "Wait a minute. About five years ago an old fellow did bring a brown mare here. A fine looking mare, and I recall he wanted some papers signed to show she had been bred to Black Knight. Fellow named Thomas. He might be your man. Lives over beyond Sand River. Just follow this road about twenty miles. Good luck, Son."

Janon's hopes rose. "Let this be the one," he said aloud. It was half a wish and half a prayer.

When he drove up to the small ranch, Janon saw a dark mare in the corral. As she lifted her head his heart beat

40

faster. There was something familiar about her, like a family resemblance. Then he saw she had a large irregularly shaped star in her forehead. His heart skipped a beat. This was the end of the trail!

He soon found Mr. Thomas, a kind-faced elderly man who listened attentively to his story. When Janon finished Mr. Thomas nodded. "That's him," he said. "Black, with a big white diamond in his forehead and fine conformation. I registered him. Hoped to race him, but had a bad year—drought and dust storms—and I had to sell him. I've been sorry ever since. When I saw the way they handled him when they loaded him I was sick. He fought them to a standstill and was half dead before they got him in the truck."

"His papers," said Janon tensely. "Have you got his papers?"

"Yes." Mr. Thomas nodded. "Those fellows never asked for them. I guess they intended to race him on the small bush tracks and make their money betting. So you've got him now? How is he?"

Janon told the story from the beginning—how they had gotten the horse, and the slow and patient work with him. Mr. Thomas listened intently.

"That's the way he always should have been handled. He was the highest-spirited horse I ever saw. Many of the really good ones are like that. They have to be handled gently or not at all."

He paused as his memory went back. "The mare out there, his dam, may not look like it now, but she was the sweetest race mare you ever saw. Not quite a stakes mare, but almost. And honest as the day is long."

"What about that stallion?" Janon said. "His sire, Black Knight."

"He was a really good race horse. Not tops, but he could have been if they had more races at a distance. He was a stayer, a real stayer. Just about got warmed up at a mile. But they want speed nowadays and they sent him out here when he couldn't get colts in California that won early. I always thought he might one day get a really good one. The blood is there. Yours might be the one."

"He beat a lot of quarter horses last week. He did it easily."

"Do you know his time, Son?"

"They said it was twenty-three seconds."

Mr. Thomas' eyes showed surprise. "Then he's got speed. Maybe more than his sire. You may have yourself a race horse—a real race horse."

Janon's face showed his delight.

"I'll get his papers," said Mr. Thomas. "I saw them the other day when I was cleaning out my desk. I almost threw

There was something familiar about her, like a family resemblance. Then he saw she had a large irregularly shaped star in her forehead. His heart skipped a beat. This was the end of the trail!

them away but something held me back. Maybe it was a hunch."

As Janon was about to leave, the precious papers safely in an inside pocket, Mr. Thomas came up to the car and laid a hand on his arm.

"Let me know how he does, Son," he said. "Maybe I can make it to the track when he starts. From the day he was foaled I always had a sort of feeling about him. As if he might be something special."

10 "As If
He Were a Hummingbird"

When Janon's father saw the boy's happiness at the success of their venture he did not have the heart to point out how rugged the road was ahead. Mr. Kendricks had made the down payment on the land as soon as Janon came back with the papers, but now he lay awake many hours at night for the ninety days before the final payment was due loomed large in his mind. Everything depended on this black horse that had but a short time ago seemed a complete outlaw. And he could not fail to notice that the blow of the whip across the black's face had its effect. He was more wary, and the complete confidence in Janon and himself was gone. Or so it seemed. Maybe it was only his imagination, but something seemed different. There was a tension in the air when he approached the horse that hadn't been there before the race.

He noticed how much time Janon spent in the corral with the black. And he could not fail to see how much time he spent stroking his head and apparently talking to him. Even from a distance he could sense how softly Janon's hand was stroking King. Yesterday he had noticed the little faded book about Rarey on a table where Janon had left it. His eye had caught the line "Stroke him as gently as if he were a hummingbird." The boy had really taken that to heart.

Well why not? Mr. Kendricks told himself as he lay awake. If that slim fearless man could walk into a stable and tame a thoroughly dangerous horse with the magic of his hands and voice, make him forget abuse and mistreatment in a matter of hours, why was anything impossible? So far Janon had been right. The horse trusted him completely before. He would again. And at last sleep came.

Janon now spent all his waking hours with the black horse. Much of the time was in the corral and when they went out for rides it was at an easy pace—nothing faster than a slow canter.

"No speed for awhile," his father had said. "That will make him forget. He's fit now and slow work will keep him in shape. Toward the last we'll have to start fast gallops again but there's plenty of time for that. Wait till you feel he's just as he was before the quarter horse race—relaxed and easy and right with you all the way."

"I'm not really worried, Dad. All I have to do if I am, is to think what Rarey did. Especially with Cruiser. That

"Stroke him as gently as if he were a hummingbird." The boy had really taken that to heart.

46

horse nearly killed a man. They had a heavy iron muzzle on him and no one dared go into his stall. If Rarey could tame a horse like that in a few hours what have we to worry about?"

"That was really amazing, Son."

"Did you read where it told how the owner gave Cruiser to Rarey and he took him back to this country? How Rarey would never part with Cruiser and said he was the most intelligent horse he had ever known? How he left money in his will to take care of Cruiser as long as he lived?"

"It's hard to believe, Son, but I know it's true. It was in all the papers. Both here and abroad."

"I read the whole book. Many times. And that's all there was to it. Just the voice and the hands. Only *for hours.* Everybody was looking for the secret. But there it is. It has to be. The time. Hours and hours."

"I'm sure you're right. I can see it in King. It shows through more every day."

"I'm sure Great-grandfather believed it!" said Janon. "He had marked many places in the book. And there were two places he had marked with a double underline."

"What were they, Son?"

" 'A true horseman should know neither fear nor anger,' and 'Stroke him as gently as if he were a hummingbird.' "

11 Mr. Thomas Again

Janon was cantering along the road a mile from home when he first noticed a car coming toward him. Not many came along that dirt road, so each was something to be noticed. As it drew close he saw it was a very old truck. When he pulled King up to wait at the side of the road he recognized Mr. Thomas at the wheel.

"So there he is," said Mr. Thomas and his face lighted up as he looked at the black horse. "He's even better than I expected. You always ride him in that saddle?"

"Yes," said Janon. "Some folks smile to see a saddle like this out here. I just tell them this isn't a broncho—it's a race horse."

"You're right, Son. And if looks mean anything he's a good one. I got to thinking about him and I had such a hankering to see him I just drove over."

"Dad will be so glad you did. He will want to thank you for the papers," said Janon. "Our place is right over there!" And he pointed to the low ranch house.

"Fine, Son. Would you mind cantering along in front of me? I'd like to see how he goes."

"I was just going back," said Janon. "We'll lead the way." He swung the black onto the road and they started off at a slow reaching gallop that kept them well ahead of the truck. When they reached the corral he pulled up and waited for it to arrive.

Mr. Thomas got out stiffly and walked over to them. His hand went out slowly and he gently stroked the black's shining neck. "He moves just as his dam used to—a little longer stride. He's bigger than she is, but the same smooth action. When you see a stride like that you know the horse can stay. Have you any plans for him?"

Mr. Thomas' kindly face and the interested look in the faded blue eyes won Janon's confidence and he poured out the whole story—their hopes and their dreams and how they had worked with the horse.

"Rarey?" he exclaimed. "You've heard of him? My father saw one of his exhibitions when he was a boy. He never forgot it. He often told me about it. How they brought in this vicious horse that two men with long ropes could hardly hold, and Rarey moving around so slim and cool putting on hobbles and the horse trying to get at him. Then when he had the horse down and helpless he went over him with his hands for an hour or more, talking to him all the time. Then he took the hobbles off and let

They started off at a slow reaching gallop that kept them well ahead of the truck.

50

the horse up and walked with him around the ring and that horse was like a family pet."

"How did he do it, Mr. Thomas? How do you suppose he ever did it?"

Mr. Thomas was thoughtful. "I've thought about it, Son. Father had the notion it was because he was closer to the horses than any one that ever lived. Understood them so well that he could talk to them as he would to another person. Really got through to them with his hands and his voice. Maybe to them he wasn't even a man— not as they had known men."

Mr. Thomas had been enthusiastically welcomed, and agreed to stay overnight. Janon was very pleased for he liked Mr. Thomas and his quiet, gentle ways. He could tell by the way he touched a horse that the older man felt as his father and he did about them. And he knew that there were many stories that he had stored in his mind of his years around horses. When the time was right he knew he would hear them.

"Your son told me about your plans and I don't think it's impossible," said Mr. Thomas at the supper table. "I was around the tracks for quite a spell and I saw a lot of horses—real good horses—and this black fellow wouldn't suffer by comparison. He's got conformation and action and his bloodlines are good enough so he could be right up there. Stamina on both sides and from what your son

52

told me he's really got speed. If he takes kindly to racing he could win a stake that would take care of your plans, I feel pretty sure."

"That's the catch," said Mr. Kendricks. "When we got him he was wild as a hawk. Trusted no one. You could see he'd been knocked around plenty. What if that had happened at a track? If they'd tried to race him and couldn't? Could we even get him near a track again?"

Mr. Thomas was silent and thoughtful. "I had one once that had gone through the mill—just like this fellow. The people I was with gave up on him but I just couldn't. Something about him got to me. Men had done that to him and it seemed only fair that men should set it straight. I was young and I asked to take over. I lived with that horse. Had a cot put in the next stall. He knew I was always there. He never called me that I didn't come. We *really* got to know each other.

"When I groomed him I found he had a very thin hide. A stiff brush drove him crazy. After I found that, nothing but a soft rag ever touched that horse. He had always hated grooming—really raised a rumpus—but now he loved it. It must have been something like Rarey's idea—that rubbing with a soft rag and me always talking to him. And it worked. But only for me. He wouldn't let anyone else near him. I had to exercise him and when they came to race him he wouldn't let a jockey up. He was a one-man horse."

"And what then?" asked Janon breathlessly.

"I was light enough but not an experienced jockey. He won a few races but only when he was much the best. I couldn't help him much. But that's the way it had to be. He wouldn't have anyone else. He was a one-man horse."

Janon sat silent and thoughtful.

12 Planning for the Race

The next day at breakfast Janon said to Mr. Thomas, "You said that horse you worked with became a one-man horse. Does that often happen?"

"With that sort of horse it does," said Mr. Thomas. "If he's been abused and then finds someone who's gentle and kind, that will be the only one he trusts."

"You think it may be that way with King? It will be only me?"

"It might be. From what I've seen I think maybe it will be."

"And I'll have to be the rider? Even in races?"

Mr. Thomas nodded.

A worried look came on Janon's face. "But I've seen pictures of those jockeys. Short stirrups—knees way up to here. I could never ride like that."

"You wouldn't have to. Jockeys didn't always ride like that. But when the style came in they all went shorter and shorter. Maybe it's all right for those short dashes but over a distance I'm sure a boy could do better with longer stirrups and a more balanced seat. But these days everyone goes to extremes. They're all so afraid of the middle of the road." He smiled at Janon. "When you're really galloping pull up enough to be over his withers—no more. Don't be afraid to be a loner. You've got a fine, natural seat on a horse. You can feel when you're with him."

"Where do you think we should go?" asked Mr. Kendricks. "What track?"

"Not Santa Anita," said Mr. Thomas. "Maybe someday, but not now. I'd say Phoenix. They're trying to build up route racing there and their closing day stake is made for your horse. A mile and a half and a ten-thousand-dollar purse. That would probably solve your problems if he could do it, wouldn't it?"

"It would," said Mr. Kendricks. "It certainly would."

"I know an old trainer there. He's as good as they come but he's never had really good horses to work with so he's never been heard of much. The black is his kind of horse. He trained my mare."

"Do you suppose he would take our horse? The way we have to do it? We'll have to take him down just before the race. We can't risk it any other way, you know. It will have to be quick, before he gets nervous at the change."

"He'll understand that," said Mr. Thomas. "I'll write

"You think it may be that way with King? It will be only me that he'll trust?"

56

him. But he knows more about a horse, just seeing him, than lots of them do handling him for a week. He'll really help, even in that short time."

Mr. Kendricks seemed relieved. "I'll certainly be obliged if he'll handle things down there."

"He will. I can guarantee that," said Mr. Thomas with conviction.

"And what shall I do to get him ready?" asked Janon anxiously. "Since we have to go down just before the race I've got to be sure he's ready to do his best."

"On the track they give them long slow gallops every day and then ask them for speed every third or fourth day. Just go along like that." Mr. Thomas paused and then added, "There was a very successful trainer who once said, 'When they look good they feel good. When they feel good they run good.' Follow that and you won't go wrong."

When Mr. Thomas was ready to leave he cast a last long look around the place. It was clear that he was reluctant to go.

"I've had such a nice time," he said earnestly. "Talking to you folks and seeing the horse again. It gets sort of lonesome off there. You get to talking to yourself for fear you'll forget how."

"You're more than welcome anytime," said Mr. Kendricks as he gripped the older man's hand. "Anytime at all. We expect you to come over and see how we're doing with the horse. Whenever you can spare the time. We've enjoyed your visit. It gets lonesome here too sometimes."

Janon watched as the old truck drove down the road throwing up a small cloud of dust.

"Isn't he nice, Dad? I'm going to miss him."

"So am I, Son. He's one of the nicest men I ever met. And interesting. You can learn plenty by listening to him."

"You know, Dad, I don't think he wanted much to leave. I hate to think of him out there all by himself."

"You noticed that? I thought I did too."

"Do you suppose, Dad, if we should get that land and more horses and all that . . ." his voice trailed off.

Mr. Kendricks laid his hand on Janon's shoulder. "Maybe something might work out. It's nice to think about."

13 The Cot in the Stable

The next day when Mr. Kendricks went into the stable for a bridle he saw a cot in front of King's stall. On a box were Janon's brush and comb and beside the cot his worn bedroom slippers. A smile came over Mr. Kendricks' face as he rubbed a hand across his eyes. He had forgotten how it was to be young—that young. How intense the feelings were and how deep they ran. He must remember not to smile or seem surprised when Janon asked permission to sleep in the stable.

Janon was out every day with King. The days that called for long slow gallops were a joy to him and apparently to the black as well, for he flowed along like a river— effortlessly as a swift running current. It was not only the smoothness of the big black's stride that delighted Janon. The feeling that he could go on forever came through to him stronger with each passing day. Mr. Thomas had said not many horses at that track had ever been tried at more than a mile and left it clear in Janon's mind that he suspected the stamina in all of them. Each day that Janon

60

galloped King he felt surer that no distance was too great for the big striding black horse. The reserve of power that he felt through his hands and knees seemed limitless.

Planning for the days that called for speed Janon had gone on foot over a half mile stretch of prairie, checking for prairie dog and gopher holes. Carrying a few thin sticks with bits of cloth tied to them he had marked these holes until he had a course that he knew was safe. By now the black knew the place as well as he. As they approached it King would begin to lean on the bit, going sideways in his eagerness. It was clear that he loved the excitement of speed. Janon's heart leaped when he felt this. Such a horse would never back away from any chance to show it. He felt in his heart that this desire, this craving for speed, would overcome any nervousness or fear. If they got him to the start he would run his race.

The joy that he and the black horse felt in galloping over the open range built up a closeness that Janon felt was stronger than ever before. Perhaps the fact that he and the horse were always together made a difference. Every morning, just as the first faint pink showed over the hills, the horse would lean over the door of his stall and nicker softly. In a moment Janon would be up and minutes later a feed tub with oats, corn and a little bran would be in King's stall. This was, for him, ham and eggs and fragrant coffee. Soon after, a cool bucket of water from the windmill pump would appear and then a forkful of hay, still smell-

ing new-mown. After such a bad interlude as he had gone through it was a good life. He was at last among friends.

Such a change must eventually iron out the scars of brutal treatment, no matter how deep, and Janon felt the change day by day. Now it was as if they were two people who were very close—brothers, almost.

Bit by bit Janon's worry about riding in the race began to lessen. Each time when they came to the stretch where he really let the black open up he pulled up on his stirrup leathers until he felt the snug tension with the stirrup at the increased speed and his more forward position in the saddle. Now he felt himself riding over the withers, light as a bird. No one needed to tell him this was the right position at speed; he could feel it through every fiber of his body. With it came a confidence that he now shared with King. He knew they were a team and felt that no one could beat them. No one!

In the days of uncertainty the time seemed to fly by, bringing ever nearer the day of trial. But now that the feeling of certainty was so strong the time dragged interminably. How Janon wished the race were tomorrow.

As they jogged back toward home with the evening sun throwing a long shadow before them they came to the

Every morning, just as the first faint pink showed over the hills, the horse would lean over the door of his stall and nicker softly.

barway that led to the land that Janon was sure would soon be theirs. There would be a gate there, and a painted sign—he could almost see it—"King of Diamonds Ranch." Over by the spring, there, were the mares and their foals. The yearlings would be over the hill down by the draw. It was only a daydream but he felt it would really come true.

14 The Trailer

The race was three days away when Janon's father said at breakfast, "I've arranged to borrow a two-horse trailer and I'm going over for it today. This afternoon we'll have to try loading him. It may be quite a job. Might take hours the first time. We've got to get an early start on Thursday. It's a long drive to Phoenix and we can't afford to be held up hours in getting the horse loaded. We've got to be sure he'll go in the trailer."

"But he's so well behaved now," said Janon. "Do you think he'll mind that?"

"Lot of horses do. Especially the first time. They're all nervous about going into an enclosed place like that. And you can't force it. If you try you're all finished. The only thing is patience. They've got to make up their own minds. Once they've done it and found no harm came from it you're set."

"How do we go about it, Dad?"

"Let him look it all over first, very thoroughly. Smell it, touch it with his nose, know what it is. Then comes the slow part. He trusts you more than anybody so I'll let you do it. You'll have to have him on a long lead shank while you stand in the trailer. Ask him to come but don't pull. You might be there for an hour, maybe much more. It's got to be his own decision. You might have a couple of carrots in your pocket to help him make up his mind at the very last—when you feel he's almost decided to go—then a little grain once he's in. But it will take patience."

"I won't mind," said Janon. "I like to be with him—just be around him."

"I know," said his father. "I can see that. And believe me that will help."

It had been a long afternoon. At first the black had refused to go near the trailer so Janon had walked him around and around it in narrowing circles, stopping occasionally to let King have a long look at it. Finally he had gotten him near enough so he could sniff at it and finally touch it with his nose. Then Janon stepped up into the trailer holding onto the very end of the lead shank. King snorted and pulled back but when he saw there was no attempt to pull him forward he stopped. So they stood for an hour, Janon talking quietly and encouragingly and the

It had been a long afternoon. At first the black had refused to go near the trailer.

66

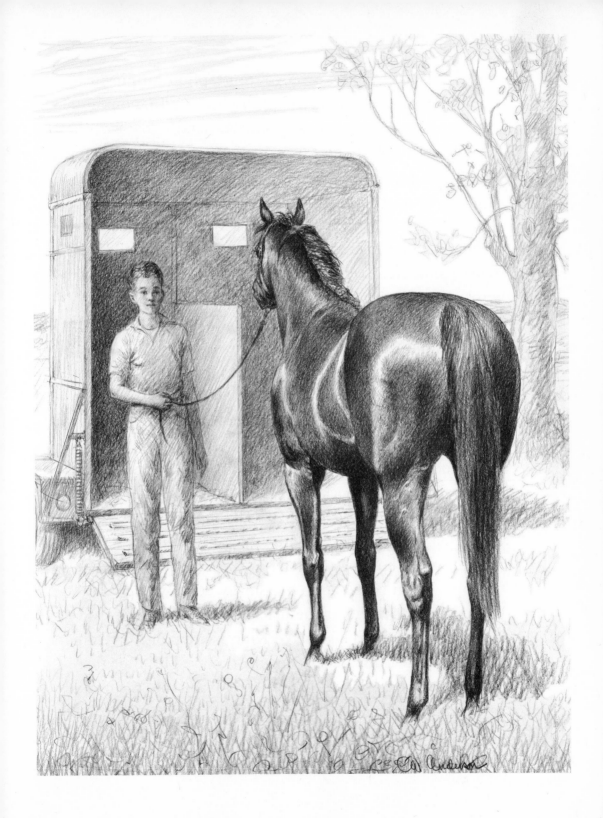

horse still eyeing the strange contraption suspiciously.

At last, a step at a time, he approached until Janon could stroke his nose with his outstretched hand. Now was the time to find out if there was really magic, real soothing power, in repeated soft, caressing strokes so light they scarcely could be felt. "As if stroking a hummingbird," Janon said to himself. Watching closely he saw the nervousness and fear replaced by a look of contentment. Janon took a slow step backward and the horse followed. More stroking and soft talk and then another step. A couple of more backward steps and Janon's back touched the front of the trailer wall. After a few moments of hesitation King followed. Now he was in. Janon felt a surge of happiness. At first he had almost despaired of ever getting the horse aboard and he knew if he failed it was the end of their hopes.

"Good boy," he said softly as he rubbed the horse's head and reached in his pocket for the carrots. For a long time they stood there as King contentedly munched his carrots and then ate the few handfuls of grain that Janon had placed in the bottom of a feed bucket.

Later Janon backed him out slowly, step by step, always with a stroking hand at the black's head. When they were again on the ground he walked King around for a few minutes and then again approached the trailer. This time there was no hesitation. The horse walked up and into the trailer with confidence.

"Wonderful, King," said Janon as he gave him a last

carrot. "Now come along and you'll have your dinner. You've earned it."

"Now I know it really works, Dad. What Rarey and The Whisperer did. Nothing else would ever have gotten King in that trailer. He remembered what happened that first time he was loaded. You could feel it all through his body. When I felt that, I thought it was hopeless."

"I was worried about it, Son. I wasn't sure you could ever do it. I got to thinking about what Mr. Thomas told me of how those fellows handled him when they were loading him. It would take a lot to ever make a horse forget that. Ordinarily he never would, for a horse has a long memory—longer than any animal I know. To think that something so simple could do that."

"I wouldn't have believed it either. Maybe I wasn't even sure till today. But today I stood there most of the afternoon stroking his head and talking to him and you could see his eye change. In an hour it had a different expression. Entirely different. You could just see he trusted you."

His father sat quietly, his expression thoughtful. Then he spoke. "It seems like magic but it's really perfectly logical. You meet a man and you find he's fair in one deal. Still you want to see more. If you find he's fair again and again you begin to trust him. That's the way it is with a horse. He's got to be convinced you won't change. And maybe all that patting and talking and kindness really gets through to him. Gets through as nothing else will."

15 On Their Way

When they were about ready to start Janon began to get tense. What if it would be different today—if King had forgotten about yesterday and his old fears and suspicion of the trailer returned. He led the black out of the stable as the sun just began to show a thin edge over the distant hills. His hand never left the horse's neck as his quiet words of encouragement kept pace. His heart lifted as he felt no tremor under his hand. King was relaxed and at ease and walked into the trailer without question. Janon went into the adjoining partition after tying King. There he planned to be during the trip—where the black could always see him and feel his touch.

They pulled out on the road that led to the big highway which went south to Phoenix. The sage showed purple in the red rays of the morning sun. Yonder skulked a coyote, and he vanished like a gray ghost into the distance. There was a small window near King's head and he seemed fascinated as the landscape slid by him with no effort on his part. With Janon beside him and his hand always on his shoulder the horse felt no nervousness but balanced himself like an experienced traveler.

Once on the big smooth highway the miles spun away behind them. There was no traffic at this early hour and the road by-passed the few widely scattered towns, so they ran for hours without a halt. At last his father pulled off the road and came to a gradual stop before a small roadside lunchroom.

"Would you like to come in and get a bite of lunch?" he asked. Janon shook his head. "I don't want to leave him. Something might upset him."

"You're right," said his father. "I'll bring you something."

Soon he reappeared with a sandwich, paper cup of milk and a piece of cake. "And here's something for King."

Janon unwrapped the pieces of sugar and the black ate them with evident pleasure. When he had finished he rubbed his head against Janon. "You're welcome," said the boy. "Glad you liked them."

When they were again on the road the country had changed. There were huge outcroppings of rock, weathered by rain and wind-driven sand to smooth, odd shapes. Many looked like strange prehistoric beasts. In the far distance they often saw cattle and herds of sheep.

"Another two hours and we'll be there," called his father. "How are you making out back there?"

"We're both a little leg weary, maybe," said Janon, "but

I think he's really interested in the country. He doesn't miss a thing."

"The good ones are always like that," said his father. "Interested and curious. Just like intelligent people. They want to know."

A little farther on and Janon felt a tell-tale bumping. His father slowed and pulled off the road. They both knew what that was. Their tires were pretty worn and one had blown out. His father got out and went to get the jack. "I probably should have changed that one," he said, "but I thought it might last the trip. You look after King and I'll tend to this. It won't take too long."

He turned back. "It would make the trip a lot easier for the horse if we could unload him and let him walk around a little. Do you think you would have any trouble loading him again if you took him off?"

"No," said Janon. "I'm sure he knows all about that, now. And he's liked the ride. He'll walk right back in."

They dropped the tail gate and Janon backed King out. He lifted his head and looked around with great interest and followed Janon eagerly as he led him away. They walked for a distance and King cropped a little grass here and there. Then he suddenly raised his head and snorted softly. Following his look Janon saw two cowboys riding toward them. Soon they drew up.

"The good ones are always like that—interested and curious. They want to know."

72

"Having trouble?" asked one. "Can we help?"

"Thanks," said Janon. "It's only a flat. Dad'll have it done in a minute."

"That's really a horse you've got there," said the cowboy admiringly. "Where are you taking him?"

They seemed very friendly so Janon told them of their plan.

"So he's a runner? He looks like one, if I ever saw one. And he starts Saturday?" He turned to his friend and said, "What do you say we go over and see him run? What's his name?"

"King of Diamonds," said Janon.

"King of Diamonds, eh? I'll bet him against the ace any time. We'll be there. Good luck."

They turned and waved when they were on the ridge before going out of sight. Janon waved back and a warm feeling came over him. Only one look and they liked King and felt he was good. He turned toward the truck with a light heart.

16 At the Track

It was after sundown when they drove into the stable area on the back stretch of the track. Janon was watching King anxiously for any signs of nervousness that would show he had been around such an area before. Evidently those fellows never got that far with him for he showed only interest and a deep-throated whinny or two showed he knew horses were around. The races were long over and the horses had been cooled out and put away. Mr. Kendricks stopped and asked a groom where Sam Boland's stable was.

"Third on your right," he said. "You'll see him sitting outside. I just spoke to him."

Evidently the trainer was expecting them for he rose and came toward them as they pulled up at the stable. "George wrote you'd be here today," he said as he shook hands. "How was the trip?"

"Easy," said Janon's father. "The horse took it well. This is my son Janon."

The trainer turned and shook hands. "Glad to meet you, Son," he said, and Janon was aware of a pair of clear gray eyes that looked at him very intently. "George told me about you in his letter," he continued. "How you've worked with the horse. Suppose you unload him and we'll put him in his stall. After that trip he's probably ready for his feed and a good deep bed of straw. It's all ready for him."

When King was off the trailer he looked around, head high and nostrils distended. He blew through them softly.

The trainer looked at him silently and intently. "Looks like George's mare," he said at last. "Bigger, though." Then he turned and led them into the stable. Janon's heart sank. He had expected more than that. Maybe Mr. Boland was disappointed in King. Perhaps the black wasn't all that he and his father had hoped.

King seemed very content in his new quarters. Occasionally he lifted his head from the feed tub in the corner and looked around. Janon's presence seemed to reassure him.

"He looks fit," said the trainer at last. "What have you been doing with him?" Janon described the long gallops and the half mile fast gallops. "Every fourth day?" he asked. "Did you really open him up?"

"Not all the way. I tried to do it as Mr. Thomas told me," answered Janon.

When King was off the trailer he looked around, head high and nostrils distended. He blew through them softly.

"George knows horses. When he said the horse belonged here I took his word for it."

"But do you think so?" asked Janon tensely. "Do you think he can do it?"

The trainer turned to him and laid a hand on his shoulder. "I forgot, Son. You've never been around the track. We never say much. What the sports writers call a great horse we only call a good one—maybe not that. I like your horse. On looks I like him better than any I've had in my stable."

Janon's spirits rose. He knew this quiet man said only what he really thought.

"There's only one thing," Janon said hesitantly. "He's used to having me around. I've been sleeping in front of his stall. In this strange stable I thought maybe he'd feel better if—"

"Of course, Son," said the trainer. "That's a good idea. He'd be looking for you. I'll have a cot put in the next stall. Anything else on your mind, Son? Anything bothering you? You'll sleep better if you get it all straight."

"I have to ride him, you know. He doesn't let anybody else up on him. I've tried to shorten my stirrups like the jockeys but I just can't ride that short. I feel all wrong."

"Don't worry. This isn't a six-furlong sprint. This is a mile and a half. You don't need to be 'a monkey on a stick' in this. Just be balanced over his withers and he'll run his race. Anything else?"

"The starting gate. He's never even seen one. Can I get him into that?"

"I thought about that, Son. I knew it might be a problem. But I found an 'out.' You know when foreign horses come over here they let them start from outside the gate since they've never seen one, either. So I spoke to the stewards and explained everything and you will start from outside the gate.

"Oh, thank you," said Janon and his gratitude shone in his face.

"You'll sleep well, now," said the trainer. "Both of you. I've reserved a room for your father in a motel just a half mile up the road so now you're both set. See you in the morning."

17 The First Time Around

All the bustle and activity around the stable as horses were saddled for workouts, rubbed down and put away was of great interest to King and Janon.

"He looks fine," said his father when he came to the stable. "Did you get any breakfast?"

"I did," said Janon. "I sure did. There's a track kitchen and you never in your life tasted such pancakes and sausage."

"It's lucky we're only a day or two here, or you'd be too heavy to ride in the race."

"Someday, maybe, but not now. I can't gain a pound. I'm just a string bean."

The trainer came up to them. "The workouts are all over. Maybe we might give your horse a look at the track. Just so he gets the feel of it."

"I'd like to," said Janon eagerly. "I'd like to get the feel of it too before tomorrow."

"I'll bring a saddle and bridle. You'd probably like to saddle him yourself."

"Just let him gallop easily," said the trainer to Janon. "If he feels like opening up when you hit that red-and-white pole let him run down to here; just a furlong, not wide open but almost."

Janon nodded and swung the black around. He could feel through his knees how much King liked this smooth, soft-cushioned surface. His stride lengthened and soon Janon realized that he must take a stronger hold on the reins for the white rail beside them streamed by and the wind whipped his hair across his eyes. Around the turn he saw the red-and-white pole and loosened his hold slightly but tightened it at once as he felt the power under him build up like a racing motor. With voice and rein he tried to ease the flying black horse but they were well around the far turn before he could pull him down enough to turn back.

Janon was worried. He knew that he had gone faster than he had intended, but King had taken over before he realized and then it was too late. Still the horse was not breathing hard and from the way he was prancing along Janon felt it had taken nothing out of him. Anxiously he studied the trainer's face as they approached him. With relief he could see that he was not upset or annoyed.

"He really wanted to run, didn't he?" he said. "He was rolling that last eighth. Was he wide open?"

"No," said Janon. "Not quite. He can let out another notch."

The trainer's eyes opened wide. "You're sure?" he said.

"Yes," said Janon. "In that quarter horse race he was going like he did that last eighth. Then I urged him and he almost ran out from under me."

The trainer whistled softly. "Some people are going to be surprised tomorrow. Mighty surprised."

"You like the way he ran?" asked Janon eagerly.

"Son," said the trainer, "do you see those men hurrying over here across the infield? They're professional clockers. They timed your horse and they're coming over to find out who he is. Look in the papers tomorrow morning and you'll know how he did."

When Janon returned from the track kitchen after breakfast the next morning one of the grooms was waiting at King's stall. He had a newspaper in his hand. "You two got as much of a writeup as a movie star," he said. "Just take a look."

The headlines on the sporting page read, "A really *dark* horse." Janon sat down on a stool and began to read.

"Here is a fairy tale that has a good chance of coming true. About three to one is quoted as the probable odds after the report of the clockers who timed this coal-black

He saw the red-and-white pole and loosened his hold slightly but tightened it at once as he felt the power under him build up like a racing motor.

82

'dark horse' yesterday morning. He was just galloping but the time the watchers showed was that of a horse really bearing down.

"Sam Boland has the horse in his charge but he disclaims credit as trainer. The horse was conditioned on the prairies of Montana by the owner, Mr. Kendricks, and his sixteen-year-old son, Janon, who bought him as an outlaw, worked with him and made him a mannerly, if spirited horse. However, since the boy, Janon, was constantly with him, sleeping in the stable near him, and riding him daily to get him in condition, he became a one-man horse. Since he will allow no one on his back but this boy, Janon Kendricks will ride him in the Phoenix Handicap today. The clockers who saw him gallop the horse yesterday said the boy was far from a green hand on a horse. One of them, Tim Murphy, who was a top rider a few years back, said, 'This boy is a natural. He rides with longer leathers and deeper in the saddle than the boys usually do, more like a steeplechase jock, but it's a seat that should fit a horse at a mile and a half. And this big black horse is a mile and a half horse. With a stride like his he'll only be galloping when the others are driving.

"From the looks of things this first-time starter, this unknown, won't be a long shot. He may even end up close to the favorites at post time. The rest of the field is pretty much an unknown quantity at a distance such as this—none of them have ever raced at more than a mile and an eighth, several have never gone more than a mile. If this big black is the stayer that the clockers seem to think we'll see more of him in the stretch. We'll be rooting for him. His name is King of Diamonds—most appropriate, for he carries a large white diamond for a star. He may well be the high card today."

As Janon put down the paper he saw Mr. Boland approaching. "You were reading that? I hope you don't mind. They kept pumping me—you know how newspaper men are—and I told them more than I intended."

"No, I don't mind. I think it's wonderful that they feel like that about King." He hesitated. "You know what that man said about my riding. Do you really think that's right? That I really suit the horse."

The trainer patted Janon on the shoulder. "Tim Murphy knows more about riding than these kids will ever learn. If you ever need a job come and see me. You can ride for me anytime."

18 Boots and Saddles

A soft nicker woke Janon. He was glad it did for he was deep in a dream that was filled with disaster. When he was awake he shook his head to clear away the web of frustration that seemed to engulf him. Now he was wide awake and he saw King's head peering at him around the corner of his stall. So he hadn't been left at the post and King hadn't gone lame. He leaped up and went for grain. Slowly the depression of the dream vanished and Janon could see from the faint rosy sky that it promised to be a perfect day. This was the day! Then he remembered what the trainer had said. That he could ride for him anytime. He had no doubts about King—only about himself. But now hope and confidence began to flow into him. This was their day! Deep inside he felt it.

There was great activity around the stable as horses were saddled for morning workouts. Janon could see that King wanted to go out with them. He had evidently enjoyed yesterday's gallop.

"Just you wait," he said to the black horse. "You'll

86

get yours this afternoon. Plenty of it. So just quiet down."

"Do you think he understands? He almost seems to," said a voice behind him.

Janon turned around quickly, a little flustered. A tall young man with glasses stood there. "I'm from the *Morning Globe*," he said. "Sam Boland gave me a story on you and the horse yesterday that my boss liked. Wanted me to get a follow-up on it. Did you see it?"

Janon nodded.

"The boss wants me to find out just how you went about curing this horse that was an outlaw. How did you do it?"

"It was mostly Father," said Janon. "He's wonderful at gentling horses. Even tough ones."

"Just what did you do?" asked the man as he took out a notebook.

Janon told the story as well as he could.

"Only that?" said the man incredulously. "Nothing else?"

"I know it sounds too simple to be true. But it works. It really works."

"You say hours? And only stroking him and talking to him gently? Was it your own idea?"

"Father always worked like that with horses but never so long. Then we found this old book that was Great-grandfather's. About a man named Rarey, James Rarey. He cured vicious horses that way. All over the world."

"Rarey? I never heard of him. How long ago was that?"

"Way back. About a hundred years, I think. I remember it said that he was asked to appear before Queen Victoria in London."

The man shook his head. "It doesn't seem possible but I believe you." He turned to the black horse who stood with his muzzle against Janon's shoulder. "And you say this fellow was really an outlaw?"

"Not really. He'd had a lot of bad treatment and he'd gotten to hate men. Didn't trust anybody. He had to forget all that."

"He certainly seems to trust you now."

"He does," said Janon simply.

"And how long did that take?" asked the man.

"About three months," answered Janon.

"And how many hours a day?" asked the man.

"All day. Every day," said Janon. "I was always with him."

The man reached out his hand and shook Janon's hand. "I don't often bet," he said, "but I'm going to today."

Janon felt strange in the silk jacket and snugly fitting white breeches. The thin boots felt queer after the heavier high-heeled ones he usually wore. The trainer stepped back and looked him over.

"You look fine," he said. "Tallest jockey around, I guess.

He had no doubts about King. This was their day!

But those long legs will come in handy on this horse. Lord, but he girths big! I had to put an extra hole in the biggest girth in the stable. And there's not an ounce of fat on him. You did a real job."

The trainer could see that the waiting was hard on the boy. Janon's face was pale and tension showed there. "Let's go over to the rail and watch this race. I've got a horse in it. We have an hour before we need to go to the paddock."

Leaning on the rail of the back stretch and listening to the trainer's comments as the horses were lining up for the start took Janon's mind off things for the moment.

"This horse I'm starting belongs to a man who just came into racing last year. He's one of these successful business men who hit it rich. The sort that always wants a winner, every time. So he bought one of those quick maturing two year olds—the kind that win early when the distances are short. He won last year at five and six furlongs so now he wanted him in this stake. A mile and an eighth. This horse will need a horse van to go more than seven furlongs. But can I tell that man so? I tried. He'll have to find out the hard way. I told him when he bought this colt that he was buying speed and nothing else. But fellows like that—they buy a sprinter and expect him to be a Derby horse."

The starter's bell clanged across the track. "There he goes," said the trainer as a chestnut horse with red-and-yellow silks dashed into the lead. "That owner's friends are probably slapping him on the back now but they'll stop when he gets over here." The chestnut was four lengths in front at the turn but as the field came thundering toward them Janon could see that lead dwindling. When they came by he was already dropping back fast.

"That's what makes a trainer old before his time," said Mr. Boland. "Trying to make a faint-hearted horse stay. Trying to pull something out of them that isn't there." He turned to Janon. "If you look in their eyes and don't see the fire that comes from the white heat inside them don't expect much."

He turned again to Janon. "Where that horse quit is just about where yours will start running."

19 The Race

Janon stood beside King ready to mount. Around him in the saddling enclosure were a dozen horses, all shining and looking fit. The colored silks of the jockeys gave a festive air to the scene that Janon could not feel. Now that the time had come, tension took over again and doubts refused to stay in the background.

The trainer's quiet voice came to him as if from a distance. "It's a big field, so stay out of the traffic. Lay well back. The ones in front the first part will be nowhere when you hit the stretch."

"How far back?" asked Janon in a shaky voice.

"Let him tell you. Only be sure he'll have something extra that you can call on at the top of the stretch. Don't use it too soon."

When Janon was in the saddle he was aware that several of the riders looked over with a grin at him. He knew he looked different in the saddle than they. "So that's the outlaw?" said one of them. "We'll tame him plenty."

"Don't mind them," said a voice beside him. "I have a

notion they'll all be eating your dust before this is over." Janon looked over and saw the outrider in his red coat beside him.

"The starter told me to give you a hand if you needed it," he said. "Would you like me to keep my horse beside you when we get to the gate?"

"Thank you," said Janon. "That would help. He's never seen a starting gate before."

"Watch it now! They're all in. Watch the chestnut with the green silks. He's the only one to worry about. Don't let him get too far ahead. Good luck."

The clanging bell sent a wild charge in its way—clods and dirt flying in all directions. At first Janon was only aware of the pounding hoofs and the cries of the jockeys. When the air cleared he could see that he and King were well back—at least fifteen lengths, maybe twenty. The black was running freely with a tremendous stride and Janon felt they were no longer losing ground. Now they were going by the stands the first time and over the roar of the crowd he heard a wild cowboy yell, "Yippee," and then "Come on, you King of Diamonds." That must be the two cowboys he had met.

Now all the panic had left him and he felt as cool as if he were out on a gallop at home. Everything was sharp and clear and his hands were steady and sure. "Easy," he said as he felt King's eagerness to catch the horses in front. Now they were on the back stretch and gradually the gap be-

tween King and the leaders had shortened. Some were dropping back already and they were coming back to him fast. A mile had done that. King was galloping strongly and Janon felt a little more drive in his stride. They were gaining fast now and he sensed King's eagerness to be with the leaders.

They were on the far turn when suddenly three of the horses seemed to collapse. They shortened stride and were all but staggering, leaving only the chestnut with the green silks in front. King swung out and passed the tired pace-setters. Still Janon kept his tight rein. He had to wait until they were around the turn and in the stretch. It was hard, for the chestnut horse was still full of run and he had to go a long way to catch him.

Now they straightened out and Janon saw the long stretch before him. Up there was the finish line. Now was the time.

"Come on, King!" he cried and his voice rose in his excitement. "Come on! Come on, Boy!"

Janon felt the added drive and power but it was not quite like it was at the end of the quarter horse race. This was the effort of a tired and game horse giving the very full of all that was in him. Yard by yard they were gaining on the chestnut. They were at his girth, his throatlatch,

"So that's the outlaw?" said one of the riders with a grin. "We'll tame him plenty."

and past! Janon saw the finish line and he did not know if it was soon enough. They were far up the track and he could not tell by the cheering who had won. Around the turn he at last eased King and gradually turned him back. His hand never left that black wet neck and his voice said over and over, "You were wonderful, Boy, just wonderful. I don't know if we did it, but you were wonderful."

Now they were cantering slowly back. As they got nearer the stands something seemed to come through the roar. Then it came clear. "King of Diamonds," he heard, and then still clearer, "King of Diamonds." So they had done it. He suddenly felt weak. He scarcely knew he was in the winner's circle or how he got there. He saw his father and Mr. Thomas side by side, and then the trainer. All as in a dream. Weakly he slid off King and leaned against him. He knew great happiness would come later but now he was tired. Very tired.

They were at his girth, his throatlatch, and past! Janon saw the finish line and he did not know if it was soon enough.

King of Diamonds Ranch

The big black horse was swinging with the easy lope of a seasoned cattle horse. Janon rocked with him, humming a little tune. "What do you think of it all, King?" he said. He waved his hand gaily at the surrounding range. "You got it for us. Aren't those nice mares out there? And those young horses. Won't we make nice saddle horses out of them! You should be proud of yourself."

Whether the black horse understood or not he seemed to carry himself a little more proudly. A gate loomed ahead and swinging overhead between the uprights was a sign. Janon sat back in his saddle and surveyed it with satisfaction and contentment. At the top was painted in handsome letters, "King of Diamonds Ranch." Below were the names:

> J. N. Kendricks
> Janon Kendricks
> George Thomas

The setting sun gilded the letters and it seemed reflected in Janon's face.